NOV   2013

Forces and Motion

LEON GRAY

Gareth Stevens
Publishing

Please visit our website, www.garethstevens.com. For a free color catalog of all our high-quality books, call toll free 1-800-542-2595 or fax 1-877-542-2596.

Library of Congress Cataloging-in-Publication Data

Gray, Leon.
Forces and motion / by Leon Gray.
    p. cm. — (Physical science)
Includes index.
ISBN 978-1-4339-9505-7 (pbk.)
ISBN 978-1-4339-9506-4 (6-pack)
ISBN 978-1-4339-9504-0 (library binding)
1. Force and energy — Juvenile literature. 2. Motion — Juvenile literature. I. Gray, Leon, 1974-. II. Title.
QC127.4 G73 2014
531.6—d23

First Edition

Published in 2014 by
Gareth Stevens Publishing
111 East 14th Street, Suite 349
New York, NY 10003

© 2014 Gareth Stevens Publishing

Produced by Calcium, www.calciumcreative.co.uk
Designed by Simon Borrough
Edited by Sarah Eason and Jennifer Sanderson

Pic credits: Cover: Shutterstock: Nejron Photo. Inside: NASA: 17, 36, 41, 42, 44; Shutterstock: AISPIX by Image Source 22, Yuri Arcurs 25r, Hung Chung Chih 45, Peder Digre 26, Max Earey 10, Iakov Filimonov 37, Germanskydiver 1, 34, 35, Gregor 19, Iofoto 9, Ivanagott 15, Jabiru 4, Matthew Jacques 20, Tomas Jasinskis 28, Justasc 16, Dmitry Kalinovsky 31, Georgios Kollidas 40, Lukiyanova Natalia/ Frenta 13, Mazzzur 18, MilanB 12, N Mrtgh 5, Mushakesa 43, Vitalii Nesterchuk 38, Nicku 14, Nomad Soul 29, Oliveromg 7, Alta Oosthuizen 21, Owl Mountain 23, Christopher Parypa 33, Pavel L Photo and Video 32, Pryzmat 24, 25l, Radu Razvan 6, Sippakorn 8, Sommthink 27, Vladimir Wrangel 11, Vasilieva Tatiana 14, Violetblue 39, Pan Xunbin 30.

Printed in the United States of America

CPSIA compliance information: Batch #CS13GS: For further information contact Gareth Stevens, New York, New York at 1-800-542-2595.

Contents

Feel the Force

Forces make things happen. They push and pull on objects, speeding them up, slowing them down, and changing their direction. The forces that push and pull on objects on Earth are the same as those that keep the planets in orbit around the sun.

Forces at Work

If you have ever taken a ride on a rollercoaster, you will know what it feels like to have forces pushing and pulling on your body. As you hurtle up and down, forces start to work. They make you feel heavier as you climb up the steep track, and lighter as you plunge down the other side. Forces push and pull on every object in the universe, from distant galaxies in outer space to the cells that make up the human body.

> You can feel the effects of a force called gravity when you take a ride on a rollercoaster.

Use the Force

Since ancient times, people have used forces to build amazing structures such as the Egyptian pyramids and Stonehenge. They also invented simple machines, such as pulleys and wheels, to make work easier. Back then, no one really understood how forces worked.

Engineers in ancient Egypt used ramps, wheels, and other simple machines to lift the heavy stone blocks used to build the pyramids.

SUPER SCIENCE FACT

Scientists measure forces in units called newtons in honor of Sir Isaac Newton. One newton is the force that accelerates 2.2 pounds (1 kg) by 3 feet (1 m) per second, each second.

Newton's Laws

In the late 1600s, the English scientist, Sir Isaac Newton, came up with three laws to describe forces and motion. Newton's Laws of Motion paved the way for modern science (see pages 14–19).

Chapter One
Moving All the Time

The world is constantly moving. Living things move around to find food. Machines, such as automobiles and planes, help people to move quicker than they can by foot. Our muscles provide the force to move our bodies around. Engines provide the force to move vehicles. Forces make things move.

Push and Pull

Forces make objects move by pushing and pulling on them. Forces work all the time. Sometimes you do not even notice them. In fact, there are many forces acting on your body right now!

Gravity

A force called gravity is pulling you down toward the center of Earth. You cannot feel it, but this invisible force is working all the time to keep your feet firmly on the ground. The ground pushes back with an equal and opposite force.

Cyclists must push harder on their pedals to cycle up a steep mountain because they are working against the force of gravity.

Out of Balance

When forces balance, you cannot feel them. The two forces cancel each other out so nothing happens. When forces do not balance, it makes objects move. Think about a tug-of-war, when two teams pull against each other on a rope. Each team tries to pull the other team forward by pulling harder on the rope. When the two pulling forces are the same, neither team moves. As one team tires, however, the two pulling forces do not balance and the other team wins.

SUPER SCIENCE FACT

Engineers study the forces acting on structures such as bridges and buildings. It is important that the forces balance perfectly so the structures do not collapse.

A tug-of-war shows how pulling forces can make things move. One team must pull harder than the other team to win the contest.

Different Forces

Different forces push and pull on objects to make them speed up or slow down. Some forces, such as friction and air resistance, are contact forces. Other forces act on objects without touching them. They include gravity and magnetism.

You can see the force of friction at work as a race car skids along the racetrack.

Friction

The force that acts on objects when they touch each other is friction. Every object, even something as smooth as a pool ball, is covered with microscopic bumps and dents. When the ball rolls along the surface of the pool table, the tiny bumps on the ball's surface rub against the bumps on the surface of the table. Eventually, the pool ball will slow to a stop.

Air Resistance

Another example of a contact force is air resistance. The air around you is not empty space; it is filled with molecules of gases such as oxygen and nitrogen. When you ride a bicycle, the molecules rub against your body and the bike. This rubbing force slows you down.

Forces at a Distance

Some forces act on objects without touching them. They are called body, or noncontact, forces and include electricity, magnetism, and gravity. These forces act on objects through invisible force fields that push and pull. An example is the magnetic field around a magnet.

SUPER SCIENCE FACT

Friction is often an unwelcome force because it slows down movement and wastes energy. But it is also very helpful. Without friction providing our feet with grip on the ground, we would not be able to stand up!

The magnetic force of a horseshoe magnet acts at a distance to attract some steel screws.

World in Motion

Forces act on objects all the time. Everything in the universe is always moving—the atoms and molecules that make up your body and even Earth itself, which constantly spins as it moves around the sun.

Fast Movers

Some things move very quickly. Earth moves around the sun at more than 67,000 miles (107,000 km) per hour. That is very quick, but light travels even faster than this. It moves at just over an incredible 186,000 miles (299,000 km) per second. Scientists think that light is the fastest thing in the universe.

The Bugatti Veyron may be the fastest car in the world—with a top speed of 253 miles (407 km) per hour—but this is just a snail's pace compared to the incredibly fast speed of light!

Slow Movers

Other things move much more slowly, so slowly that you do not notice them. A good example is Earth's continents. These giant landmasses are moving all the time, floating on a "sea" of molten rock beneath Earth's surface. But they are moving very slowly—on average, around 1 inch (2.5 cm) every year.

Muscle Movement

Have you ever wondered how you move? Muscles provide the force to move our bodies. They pull on your bones to move your arms and legs so you can jump up in the air, move a chess piece, and sprint along a running track. Large muscles have more pulling force than smaller muscles. This is why bodybuilders can lift much heavier objects than other people.

The strong, powerful muscles of an athlete provide the force to power him along the running track.

Chapter Two

Understanding Forces

The ancient Greeks were the first people to study forces. The Greek scientist Aristotle came up with the idea that forces push and pull on objects to make them move. It took another 1,600 years for scientists to take the next major step toward understanding forces.

When Galileo rolled a ball down a ramp, he found that gravity acted on the ball to speed up its movement.

Galileo's World

Italy's Galileo Galilei studied Aristotle's ideas and found that he had made some mistakes. Aristotle thought that forces always push and pull on things to make them move, but he was wrong. Galileo found that moving objects will move forever, but other forces speed them up or slow them down.

Constant Motion

Galileo tested his idea by rolling a ball down a ramp. He found that it moved faster and faster because a force (gravity) made the ball speed up. When he rolled a ball along a flat surface, the ball rolled along at the same speed, but eventually stopped. Galileo realized that the ball stopped because a force (friction) slowed it down—otherwise it would keep moving forever.

Dropping Cannonballs

Galileo did another experiment to test his ideas about forces and motion. He took cannonballs of different weights and dropped them off the Leaning Tower of Pisa. All the cannonballs hit the ground at the same time. Galileo proved that a force (gravity) pulls all objects down at the same rate no matter how heavy or light each object is.

SUPER SCIENCE FACT

In Galileo's time, religious people believed that God put Earth at the center of the universe. Galileo used his knowledge of forces and motion to suggest that Earth moves around the sun. When Galileo printed his ideas in a book, he was jailed for the rest of his life.

Galileo tested his ideas about the force of gravity by dropping cannonballs off the Leaning Tower of Pisa.

Newton's Universe

Many people think that Isaac Newton is one of the greatest scientists who ever lived. His ideas changed the way people thought about the world around them.

As a boy, Newton did not take much interest in science. All this changed in 1661, when he went to study at Cambridge University.

Clockwork Universe

Isaac Newton was born in England in 1642, in the same year that Galileo died. He studied the work of Galileo and other scientists and used mathematics to combine all their ideas into a few simple laws. Newton's laws worked for every object in the universe, which he described as a giant "clockwork machine."

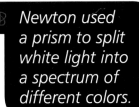

Newton used a prism to split white light into a spectrum of different colors.

Best Seller

Newton wrote his ideas down in a book, called *Principia*, which was published in 1687. In the first part of his book, Newton explained that three basic laws determine how objects move when forces act on them (see pages 16–17). Newton then used these laws to prove that gravity also makes the planets move around the sun (see pages 18–19).

Work on Light

Newton also discovered that white light consisted of different colors. He suggested that light was made up of particles—an idea that Albert Einstein then proved some 200 years later.

SUPER SCIENCE FACT

Newton was a brilliant inventor as well as a scientist. In 1668, he used a mirror to build an extremely accurate telescope to study the universe. He even invented the cat flap so his pet cat could get in and out of his front door without him having to open the door himself!

Laws of Motion

Newton's three Laws of Motion describe how things move. They are the same for all moving objects—from automobiles traveling along a freeway to the planets moving around the sun.

First Law of Motion

The First Law of Motion says that an object will stay still or keep on moving at the same speed, unless a force acts on it. This law is about inertia. If you throw a baseball up in the air, it will fall back down. Forces act on the ball as soon as you throw it. Air resistance slows the ball down, and gravity pulls it back toward the ground.

When you throw a baseball, the muscles in your arm provide the force to accelerate it through the air.

Second Law of Motion

Newton's Second Law of Motion says that forces make objects accelerate. It can be written as:

Force (F) = mass (m) x acceleration (a)

Bigger forces make objects accelerate more quickly. The harder you throw a baseball, the farther it will go. It also means more force is needed to make heavy objects accelerate. Try throwing a cannonball instead of a baseball!

Third Law of Motion

Newton's Third Law of Motion says that for every reaction there is an equal, but opposite, reaction. When you throw a baseball up into the air, there is the force of your hand on the ball. The same force comes from the ball pushing on your hand— in the opposite direction.

You can see Newton's Third Law of Motion at work when a rocket launches into space.

SUPER SCIENCE FACT

In his Third Law of Motion, Newton explained how rockets work—hundreds of years before they were invented. The force of the rocket's burning gases are balanced with, or equal to, the force of the rocket moving forward.

17

Newton and Gravity

Before Newton, no one knew how or why the planets moved. Religious people thought it was the work of the gods, but Newton used his knowledge of math to figure out the truth.

Isaac Newton came up with his ideas about gravity when he saw an apple falling from a tree in his orchard.

Apple Tree
One story suggests that Newton was sitting in his family's orchard and saw an apple fall from a tree. He wondered if the force that made the apple fall down might be the same force that made the planets move around the sun.

Force of Attraction

Newton proved that gravity pulled the planets toward the sun in the same way that it pulled the apple to the ground. This force of attraction kept the planets in oval-shaped paths, or orbits, around the sun. Newton then invented a new branch of mathematics called calculus to figure out the shape and speed of these orbits.

Law of Gravitation

Newton found that the force of gravitational attraction between two objects depends on how heavy the objects are and how far away they are from each other. Heavy objects have a much stronger gravitational force of attraction than light objects. But if the two objects are far apart, the force of gravity is much weaker.

Newton used math to prove that gravity keeps the moon in orbit around Earth.

SUPER SCIENCE FACT

Gravity causes the rise and fall of the tides. As the moon moves around Earth, the moon's gravity pulls at the water from the oceans directly below it. This creates a high tide. Another high tide occurs on the other side of Earth where there is less gravity, and so the water bulges outward.

19

Chapter Three
Simple Machines

Long before Galileo and Newton, people had been using simple machines such as ramps, wheels, levers, pulleys, and gears to help overcome forces and make it easier for people to move objects.

Ramps and Wedges

One of the first simple machines was the ramp, or inclined plane. Ramps were used thousands of years ago to lift the huge stone blocks needed to build ancient monuments such as Stonehenge. Today, ramps have many uses, ranging from screws to zippers.

Prehistoric people used ramps and wedges to raise the stone blocks of Stonehenge into position.

A mountain road is a perfect example of an inclined plane at work. The road winds up and down across the mountain, making it easier for people to drive up the steep slope.

A simple wood screw is a ramp wrapped around a central shaft.

Little Effort, Large Effect

Like all machines, ramps increase the effect of forces so that a small effort produces a large effect. The force needed to drag a heavy stone block along a ramp is much less than the force needed to lift it straight up.

Mechanical Advantage

The ramp gives a "mechanical advantage" because it increases the pulling force. However, you need to drag the block over a longer distance to lift the block the same height. Increasing the distance increases the mechanical advantage, but it takes longer to lift the load.

Ramps at Work

Bolts and screws use "hidden" ramps in the form of the winding thread. Only a small force is needed to tighten the screw. The binding force of the screw and the wood is much stronger. Zippers also use ramps to zip up rows of interlocking teeth. The ramp is in the zip slide, which forces the teeth to open and close with little force.

The Wheel

Have you ever wondered why so many vehicles have wheels? Bicycles, cars, trains, and airplanes all use their wheels to roll along the ground. Many machines also have wheels to make their jobs easier to do.

The First Wheel

People who made pottery invented the first wheel in around 3500 BC. They used a turntable called the potter's wheel to shape clay into bowls and pots. Eventually, someone used wheels as rollers to make it easier to transport heavy loads.

Why Wheels Work

Sliding a heavy box over the floor creates a lot of friction, so it is hard to move. Rolling the box on wheels reduces friction because only a tiny part of each wheel touches the ground at any one time. This makes the wheel an efficient way of moving something.

The wheels used to move vehicles, such as cars and bicycles, developed from the potter's wheel, which is used to shape clay into pots.

Wheels and Axles

People first used wheels and axles on vehicles such as horse-drawn carts. An axle is a rod that connects two wheels. At first, the wheels rolled around a fixed axle, which was attached to the cart. But this created friction as the wheels rolled around the axle. People then invented the rolling axle, where the axle and wheels turned together to reduce friction.

The huge wheels of this truck have treads to roll over loose ground.

SUPER SCIENCE FACT

One of the earliest uses of wheels in machines was the waterwheel. This used the power of moving water to turn a wheel to grind grain. Today, people also use wheels in machines ranging from conveyors to cranes.

Levers

Every time you open a door, use a pair of tweezers, or sit on a seesaw, you are using a lever. Levers work by magnifying and reducing forces to make tasks easier to do.

Different Classes of Lever

All levers consist of a solid part, such as a bar or handle, that turns around a fixed point called the fulcrum. Levers are grouped into three different "classes."

Class 1 Lever

A crowbar is a simple class 1 lever. In class 1 levers, the fulcrum is in the middle. The lifting force applied at one end of the lever is magnified at the other end.

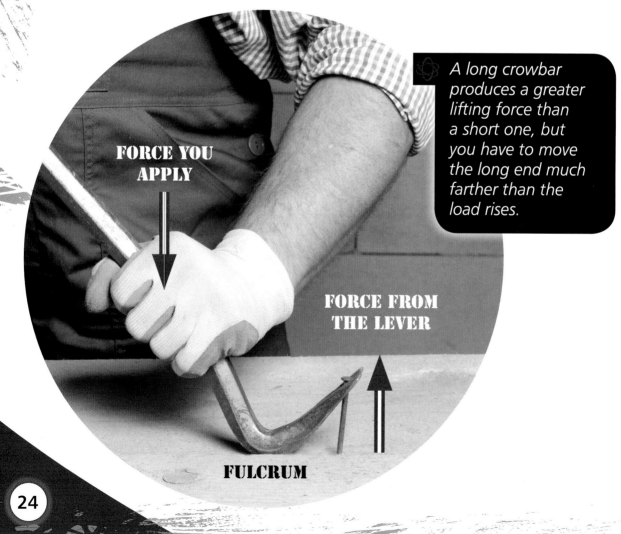

FORCE YOU APPLY

FORCE FROM THE LEVER

FULCRUM

A long crowbar produces a greater lifting force than a short one, but you have to move the long end much farther than the load rises.

Class 2 Lever

A wheelbarrow is a simple class 2 lever. It magnifies the lifting force from your arms to pick up heavy loads. In this case, the fulcrum is at one end of the lever, and the lifting force is at the other end. This creates a magnified force to lift the load in the middle of the lever.

Class 3 Lever

A pair of tweezers is a simple class 3 lever. The tweezers reduce the force from your fingers to pick up small, delicate objects. In this type of lever, you apply the force in the middle of the lever. The fulcrum is at one end of the lever and the load is at the other end.

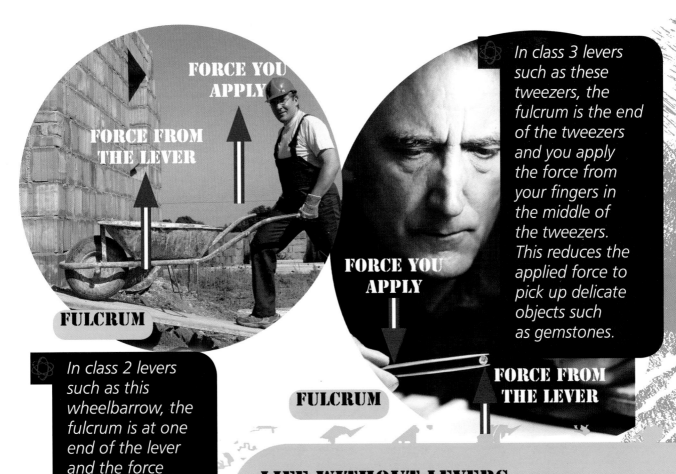

FORCE YOU APPLY

FORCE FROM THE LEVER

FULCRUM

In class 2 levers such as this wheelbarrow, the fulcrum is at one end of the lever and the force you apply is at the other end. This creates a magnified force to lift the heavy load in the middle of the lever.

In class 3 levers such as these tweezers, the fulcrum is the end of the tweezers and you apply the force from your fingers in the middle of the tweezers. This reduces the applied force to pick up delicate objects such as gemstones.

FORCE YOU APPLY

FULCRUM

FORCE FROM THE LEVER

LIFE WITHOUT LEVERS

We use levers all the time, often without knowing it. The human body contains many levers—our arms, legs, hands, and feet all help us to do jobs by magnifying and reducing forces.

Pulley Power

All pulleys consist of a length of rope wrapped around one or more wheels. These simple machines are used to lift heavy loads.

Archimedes' Pulley

A story tells of the Greek scientist, Archimedes, who used a pulley to lift a ship without any help. This story may be far-fetched, but it shows that pulleys can be used to lift heavy objects with little effort.

One Wheel

A simple pulley has one wheel with a rope wrapped around it. Pulling on one end of the rope lifts the load on the other end of the rope. A simple pulley does not magnify the lifting force. To do this, you need a compound pulley.

Two Wheels

Compound pulleys lift large loads because the lifting force moves farther than the load. In a compound pulley with two wheels, it takes half as much effort to lift the load, and the lifting force moves twice as far.

A simple pulley is used to hoist a flag up a flagpole.

The problem with pulleys is that some of the lifting force is wasted because of friction between the rope and the pulley wheels. Another problem is the weight of the pulleys themselves, which reduces the lifting force.

Cranes lift heavy objects using a steel cable wrapped around a compound pulley. Each loop of the cable magnifies the lifting force of the crane.

Pulleys in Action

Cranes lift and move heavy objects using a steel cable wrapped around a compound pulley. The pulley hangs off the main arm of the crane, called the jib. Each loop of the cable in the pulley magnifies the lifting force of the crane so it can lift heavy objects.

27

Gears

Gears are wheels with interlocking teeth that increase or decrease forces. Gears can also be used to change the speed and direction of motion. There are four main types of gear: bevel, rack-and-pinion, spur, and worm.

How Gears Work

If the first gearwheel has more teeth than the second gearwheel, the second wheel turns faster but with less force. If the second wheel has more teeth, it turns slower than the first gearwheel but with more force.

Bevel Gears

Bevel gears can be found in hand drills. These gears have two gearwheels that interlock at an angle to change the direction of movement.

Rack-and-Pinion Gears

Without rack-and-pinion gears, we would not be able to steer cars! Rack-and-pinion gears have a toothed wheel that runs along a sliding toothed rack. They change the rotation of the gear into movement along a straight line.

Power tools such as drills use gears to increase and decrease the turning force of an electric motor to drill through different materials.

Spur Gears

Spur gears are two interlocking gearwheels. These gears are used to increase and decrease forces.

Worm Gears

Worm gears have a toothed gearwheel that fits onto a cylindrical thread. They are used to tighten the strings on musical instruments.

Cycling Made Easy

You can see gears in action on bicycles. The large gearwheels near the pedals are called chain rings. A chain connects the chain rings to smaller gearwheels, called cogs, on the rear wheel. Choosing the right combination of gears makes cycling easier and faster.

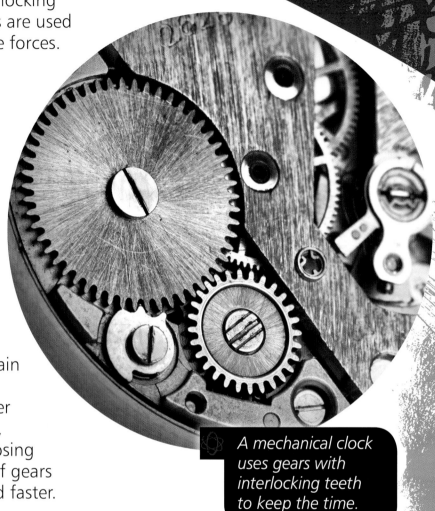

A mechanical clock uses gears with interlocking teeth to keep the time.

LIFE WITHOUT GEARS

It is hard to imagine life without gears. Vehicles use gears to make traveling easier, faster, and more efficient. Countless machines also need gears to work—everything from clocks and conveyor belts to washing machines and wristwatches.

Chapter Four

Forces and Energy

Forces change the way objects move, but you need energy to make this happen. Energy exists in many different forms and can change from one form to another. Forces often occur when energy changes from one form to another.

> Houseflies use friction to climb up walls. Each fly foot is covered with tiny hairs, which increase the friction between the foot of the fly and the wall.

Friction Force
Friction is the force that resists the movement of objects when they touch each other (see pages 8–9). There are two main forces at work when you try to move objects: static friction and sliding friction.

Static and Sliding Friction

Static friction is the stronger of the two forces. Static friction makes it hard to move a heavy object that is at rest (not moving), such as a heavy stone block on the ground. Sliding friction has an effect when an object starts moving. It is easier to push a heavy object when it is already moving, because sliding friction is weaker than static friction.

Wasting Energy

Friction wastes energy. In a perfect system, all the effort you put into the system should be transferred into movement. Friction wastes some of this effort. You can feel this wasted effort when you rub your hands together very quickly. Your hands become hot if you rub them hard enough, because friction wastes some of the rubbing force and turns it into heat.

It is important to put oil into a car engine. Oil lubricates the moving parts and stops the engine from overheating.

G-Force

Gravity is the force of attraction between every object in the universe. This invisible force is acting on your body all the time, pulling you down to Earth's surface and stopping you from flying off into space.

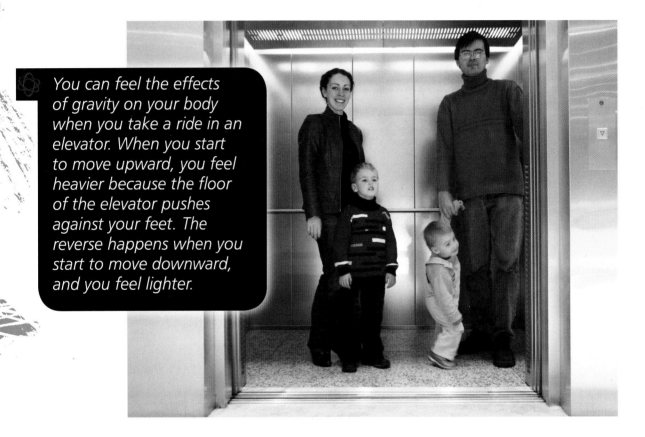

You can feel the effects of gravity on your body when you take a ride in an elevator. When you start to move upward, you feel heavier because the floor of the elevator pushes against your feet. The reverse happens when you start to move downward, and you feel lighter.

Measuring Mass

Everything has a constant mass. Mass is a measure of the amount of material an object contains. Your body has a fairly constant mass, depending on how much you eat and how much you exercise.

What Do I Weigh?

Weight is a measure of the force of gravity acting on your mass. On the moon, your mass is the same as it is on Earth, but your weight is around one-sixth as much. Gravity on the moon is less than it is on Earth, because the moon has less mass.

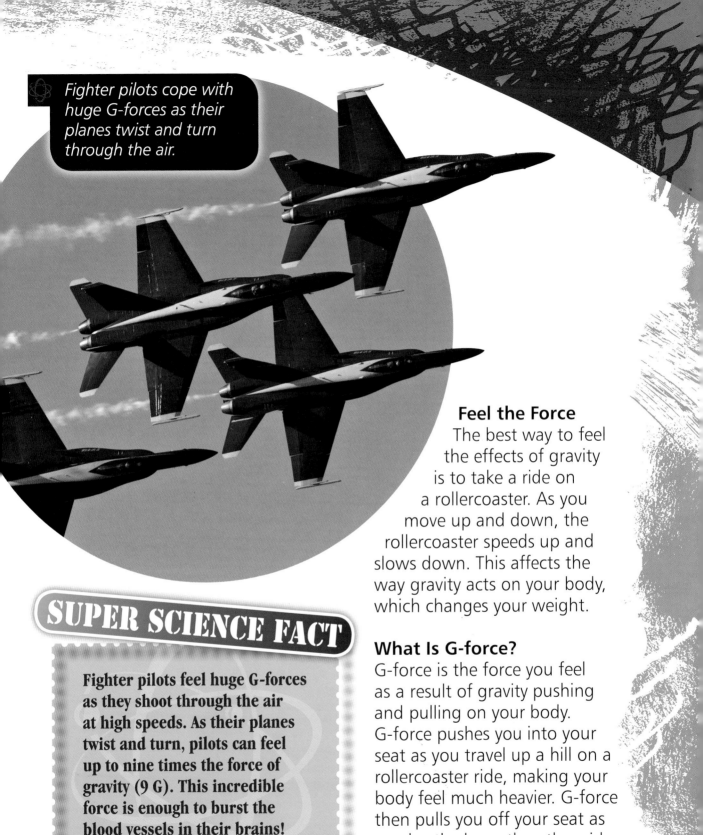

Fighter pilots cope with huge G-forces as their planes twist and turn through the air.

Feel the Force

The best way to feel the effects of gravity is to take a ride on a rollercoaster. As you move up and down, the rollercoaster speeds up and slows down. This affects the way gravity acts on your body, which changes your weight.

What Is G-force?

G-force is the force you feel as a result of gravity pushing and pulling on your body. G-force pushes you into your seat as you travel up a hill on a rollercoaster ride, making your body feel much heavier. G-force then pulls you off your seat as you hurtle down the other side of the hill, making your body feel lighter.

Free Fall

Gravity acts on our bodies all the time. Usually we do not notice it because the ground under our feet balances the effects of gravity. You can feel the full force of gravity by jumping out of an aircraft.

Ready, Jump!

As soon as you jump out of the plane, gravity accelerates your body toward Earth. In just a few seconds, your body accelerates to around 60 miles (100 km) per hour. As you fall, your body rubs against the molecules that make up the air. This creates air resistance, or drag, which acts against gravity.

Jumping out of an airplane is a good way to learn about the effects of gravity.

Terminal Velocity

After around 10 seconds of free fall, the forces of gravity and drag balance. Your body stops accelerating and you plummet toward Earth at the same speed, called the terminal velocity. This is Newton's First Law of Motion in action—a moving object will continue moving at the same speed unless a force acts on it.

Speeding Up

The terminal velocity of a falling object depends on its shape and weight. A typical adult skydiver falls at around 120 miles (200 km) per hour. To create more drag, skydivers stretch out their arms and legs.

A skydiver reaches terminal velocity when the force of gravity balances the force of drag.

SUPER SCIENCE FACT

The world's highest skydive took place in October 2012, when Austria's Felix Baumgartner leaped from a balloon 24 miles (40 km) above Earth's surface. Baumgartner reached a terminal velocity of 725 miles (1,160 km) per hour as he plummeted through the thin air of Earth's upper atmosphere.

Moving in Circles

If you have ever been on a loop-the-loop rollercoaster, you will have felt a very strong force pushing you back into your seat as you loop the loop. This force, called centripetal force, stops you from falling out of your seat, but only if the rollercoaster is moving fast enough!

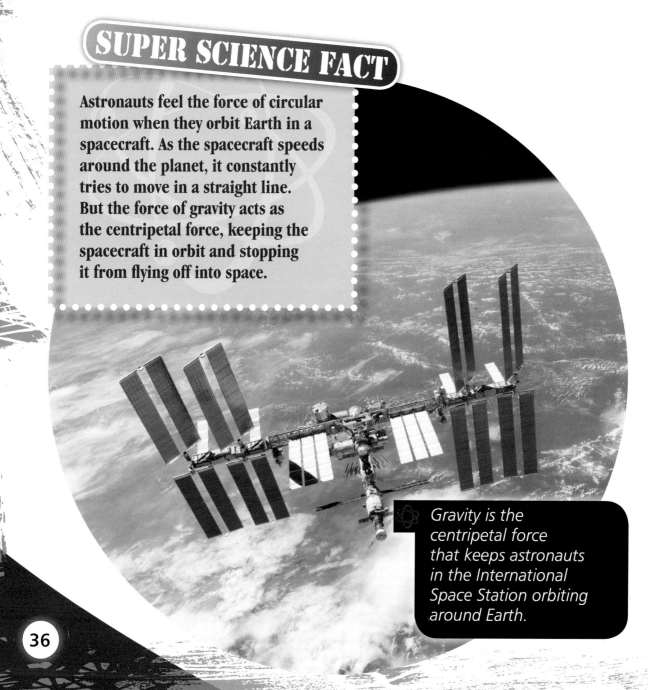

SUPER SCIENCE FACT

Astronauts feel the force of circular motion when they orbit Earth in a spacecraft. As the spacecraft speeds around the planet, it constantly tries to move in a straight line. But the force of gravity acts as the centripetal force, keeping the spacecraft in orbit and stopping it from flying off into space.

Gravity is the centripetal force that keeps astronauts in the International Space Station orbiting around Earth.

A laboratory centrifuge spins at high speed to separate mixtures of things, such as blood cells from the lighter plasma in blood.

Centripetal Force

Centripetal force acts on any object that moves in circles. You can feel the effect of this force while riding on a merry-go-round. As you spin around, your body keeps trying to move in a straight line. This is due to Newton's First Law of Motion (see pages 16–17). Your body appears to feel an outward force, called centrifugal force, which pushes you off the merry-go-round.

Deceptive Forces

Centrifugal force does not really exist. The true force is centripetal force, which pulls you in toward the center of the merry-go-round to keep you moving in a circle. This force acts through your body to keep you on the ride. Without it, you would fly off in a straight line.

Forces in Action

Many different machines make use of centripetal force. For example, washing machines use centripetal force to separate the water from wet clothes.

Energy Transfer

Energy is the ability to make things happen. Without it, there would be no forces to push and pull on objects to make them move.

Types of Energy

Energy exists in many different forms. It can never be destroyed—it just changes from one form to another.

- Chemical energy is the energy trapped inside molecules such as oil and food.
- Electrical energy is the energy that comes from the movement of electrons through materials such as metals.
- Heat energy is the energy that comes from the tiny vibrations of atoms and molecules.
- Kinetic energy is the energy things have because they are moving. Objects have more kinetic energy when they move faster.
- Light energy is the energy from sunlight and man-made sources of light.
- Nuclear energy is the energy trapped inside atoms.
- Potential energy is the energy you gain when you climb a hill or stretch an elastic band.

Potential energy turns into kinetic energy when you bungee jump.

Your muscles turn the chemical energy locked away inside food into kinetic energy so you can move around.

Energy Changes

The energy you use to swim or run around a soccer field is kinetic energy. Plants absorb the heat and light energy from the sun to make food. In turn, this provides food for other animals, including people. When you eat plants and meat, your muscles convert the chemical energy in the food into kinetic (movement) energy.

SUPER SCIENCE FACT

Energy is measured in units called joules (J) in honor of the Scottish scientist James Joule, who established the link between different forms of energy.

Chapter Five

Fundamental Forces

Newton's Laws of Motion work for most moving objects, but they do not work when objects start to move at speeds approaching the speed of light. Albert Einstein recognized this in his theories of relativity.

Albert Einstein developed a theory called relativity to describe objects moving at the speed of light.

Speed of Light

Nothing can travel faster than the speed of light. Light travels through space at an incredible 186,282 miles (299,792 km) per second.

Strange Light

Imagine you could travel 1 mile (1.6 km) per second slower than the speed of light. You might think you could catch the light. In fact, light still moves away from you at over 186,282 miles (299,792 km) per second! If the speed of light never changes, Einstein figured out that something else must change to make up for it. He used complex math to show that space shrinks and time slows down when objects travel close to the speed of light.

Einstein and Gravity

Einstein expanded his ideas to explain how gravity affects space and time. He suggested that gravity is not really a force but a "warping" of space and time. Imagine space and time as a rubber sheet stretched out over a vast area. The mass of an object, such as a planet, bends the rubber sheet, so anything that moves near it will be attracted to it. This attraction is the "force" of gravity.

Light from stars in the Messier Galaxy takes 47 million years to reach the surface of Earth.

41

Invisible Forces

Scientists use machines called particle accelerators to accelerate the tiny particles found inside atoms at near-light speeds. They hope these experiments will help them to understand the forces that hold the universe together.

This image shows the results of a particle collision inside the Large Hadron Collider near Geneva, Switzerland.

Particle Accelerators

Einstein's theories of relativity show that nothing can travel faster than the speed of light. Using particle accelerators, scientists can accelerate particles up to 99 percent of the speed of light and then smash them together. The force of these collisions creates a shower of new particles.

Predicting Einstein

The results of these particle collisions show that Einstein's theories of relativity are correct. Einstein used math to show that mass can change into energy in his famous equation $E=mc^2$. When particles smash into each other, they change into new particles. This proves that mass and energy are two forms of the same thing. Einstein also showed that the mass of an object increases as it approaches the speed of light. Scientists have measured the mass of particles inside accelerators and found this to be true, too.

 The strong and weak nuclear forces keep the protons inside the nucleus of an atom.

Fundamental Forces

The experiments inside particle accelerators have shown that there are four fundamental forces: electromagnetism, gravity, the strong nuclear force, and the weak nuclear force. All other forces come from these fundamental forces.

LIFE WITHOUT FUNDAMENTAL FORCES

The universe would collapse if fundamental forces did not exist. The strong and weak nuclear forces bind the nuclei of atoms together, while electromagnetism holds atoms together to form molecules. Gravity is the weakest fundamental force, but it works on a bigger scale, holding every object in the universe together.

Force for the Future

In the last few hundred years, scientists have begun to understand how forces work. Science is moving forward very quickly, so who knows what more we might discover about forces and motion in the future.

Forces in Space

Another interesting area of research involves studying forces and motion in space. For example, scientists are studying the effects of zero gravity on the human body to see if people could eventually live in space.

Beating Friction

Friction is the natural way to slow down something. Since friction makes machines and vehicles waste energy, scientists and inventors are always looking for ways to beat it. For example, they have made trains that "float" on a magnetic field to reduce friction between the wheels and the track. These trains are called maglev trains, which is short for magnetic levitation.

Astronauts need to exercise in the weightlessness of space to stay fit and healthy.

Grand Unified Theory

Before he died, Einstein worked on a new theory to unite the fundamental forces. He called his idea the "Grand Unified Theory." Einstein did not succeed in his quest. Today, many scientists are still working to resolve Einstein's last great mathematical problem.

Maglev trains are very fast, speeding up to 360 miles (580 km) per hour, but they are also very expensive to build. There are only two working maglev train lines in the world—one in Japan and the other in China.

Maglev trains beat the force of friction by "floating" on a magnetic track.

Glossary

acceleration how quickly an object speeds up or slows down

air resistance the force that acts on things as they travel through the air. Air resistance is also called "drag."

atoms the tiny particles that make up everything in the universe

axle a rod passing through the center of a wheel or wheels

cells the basic units of matter found in all living organisms

centrifuge a machine that spins at high speed to separate mixtures of things

centripetal force the force that keeps an object moving in a circle

electricity the flow of electrons through an object

energy the ability to do work

free fall falling through the air without a parachute or similar device so that the only force acting is gravity

friction the force that opposes motion when one object moves over another object

fulcrum the pivot point of a lever

G-force the force equal to the force of gravity. For example, 5 G is a force five times the force of gravity.

gravity the force of attraction between two or more objects

inertia the tendency of an object to continue staying still or moving at the same speed

International Space Station an artificial satellite that is used as an international research center

lubricant a substance, such as oil, used to reduce the effects of friction

magnetism the property of some materials, such as iron and nickel, to push and pull on similar materials

mass an amount of matter in an object

mechanical advantage the measure of the force achieved by using a tool, mechanical device, or machine system

molecules combinations of two or more atoms

orbit the curved path of one object, such as a planet, around another object, such as the sun

particle accelerators machines used to accelerate tiny particles at speeds approaching the speed of light

plasma the clear, liquid part of blood, made up mostly of water and proteins

relativity the theories of Albert Einstein, which link the properties of space, time, gravity, and the speed of light

speed how fast an object is moving

terminal velocity the speed of an object in free fall when the force of gravity pushing down on the object equals the drag force pushing up

weight the force of gravity pushing down on an object's mass

For More Information

Books

Dicker, Katie. *Science Detective Investigates Forces and Motion*. London, UK: Wayland, 2011.

Duke, Shirley Smith. *Let's Explore Science: Forces and Motion at Work*. Vero Beach, FL: Rourke Publishing, 2011.

Firth, Alex. *Forensic Science*. London, UK: Usborne, 2007.

Hammond, Richard. *Can You Feel the Force?* London, UK: Dorling Kindersley, 2006.

Orr, Tamra. *Science Made Simple Motion and Forces*. New York, NY: Rosen Central, 2011.

Websites

"From Apples to Orbits: The Gravity Story" has lots of information about gravity. Learn about its history, how it affects humans, or try some fun activities at:
library.thinkquest.org/27585

Learn about the solar system or take a tour of Mars and the stars. The Science Website includes a virtual globe and information about gravity and inertia at:
www.sciencemonster.com

Learn about friction by trying some great activities from the Science Museum of Minnesota at:
www.sci.mus.mn.us/sln/tf/f/friction/friction.html

Index